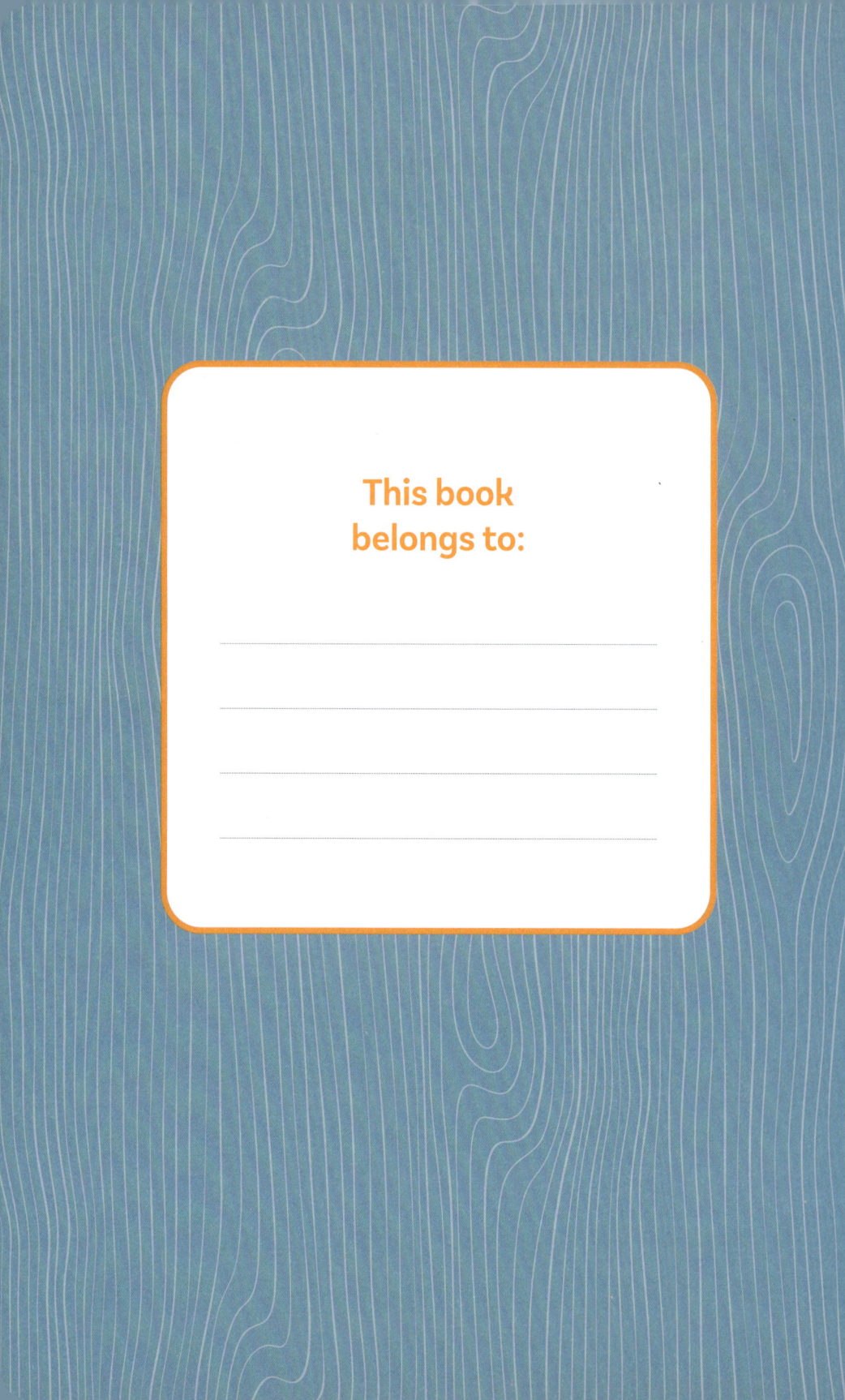

This book belongs to:

The Birder's
LOGBOOK

A Seek-and-Sticker Book
for Budding Ornithologists

PETER PAUPER PRESS, INC.
RYE BROOK, NEW YORK

Bird Checklist A–Z

As you spot the **100 birds** in this book, check off their names here! Next to each bird's name is the page number where you can find its profile.

- [ ] American Coot ... 40
- [ ] American Crow ... 24
- [ ] American Goldfinch ... 20
- [ ] American Kestrel ... 33
- [ ] American Redstart ... 17
- [ ] American Robin ... 12
- [ ] American Wigeon ... 39
- [ ] Bald Eagle ... 33
- [ ] Baltimore Oriole ... 27
- [ ] Barn Swallow ... 28
- [ ] Barred Owl ... 35
- [ ] Belted Kingfisher ... 36
- [ ] Black-and-white Warbler ... 17
- [ ] Black-capped Chickadee ... 13
- [ ] Black-crowned Night Heron ... 42
- [ ] Black-headed Grosbeak ... 23
- [ ] Blue Jay ... 23
- [ ] Bonaparte's Gull ... 44
- [ ] Brewer's Blackbird ... 26
- [ ] Brown Creeper ... 15
- [ ] Brown-headed Cowbird ... 26
- [ ] Bufflehead ... 40
- [ ] Bushtit ... 14
- [ ] Canada Goose ... 37
- [ ] Carolina Chickadee ... 14
- [ ] Cedar Waxwing ... 27
- [ ] Common Grackle ... 25
- [ ] Common Raven ... 24
- [ ] Common Tern ... 44
- [ ] Common Yellowthroat ... 18
- [ ] Cooper's Hawk ... 32
- [ ] Dark-eyed Junco ... 20
- [ ] Double-crested Cormorant ... 41
- [ ] Downy Woodpecker ... 29
- [ ] Eastern Bluebird ... 12
- [ ] European Starling ... 28
- [ ] Golden-crowned Kinglet ... 18
- [ ] Gray Catbird ... 25
- [ ] Great Blue Heron ... 41
- [ ] Great Egret ... 42
- [ ] Great Horned Owl ... 34
- [ ] Green Heron ... 42
- [ ] Hairy Woodpecker ... 30
- [ ] Hermit Thrush ... 12
- [ ] Herring Gull ... 44
- [ ] House Finch ... 21
- [ ] House Sparrow ... 20
- [ ] House Wren ... 16
- [ ] Indigo Bunting ... 22
- [ ] Killdeer ... 36
- [ ] Least Sandpiper ... 37
- [ ] Mallard ... 38
- [ ] Marsh Wren ... 16
- [ ] Merlin ... 34
- [ ] Mountain Bluebird ... 13
- [ ] Mourning Dove ... 29
- [ ] Northern Cardinal ... 21
- [ ] Northern Flicker ... 30
- [ ] Northern Harrier ... 32
- [ ] Northern Mockingbird ... 25
- [ ] Northern Pintail ... 39
- [ ] Northern Shoveler ... 39
- [ ] Osprey ... 34
- [ ] Peregrine Falcon ... 33
- [ ] Pied-billed Grebe ... 41
- [ ] Pileated Woodpecker ... 30
- [ ] Pine Siskin ... 21
- [ ] Red-bellied Woodpecker ... 31
- [ ] Red-breasted Merganser ... 40
- [ ] Red-breasted Nuthatch ... 15
- [ ] Red-tailed Hawk ... 32
- [ ] Red-winged Blackbird ... 26
- [ ] Ring-billed Gull ... 43
- [ ] Rock Pigeon ... 29
- [ ] Rose-breasted Grosbeak ... 23
- [ ] Ruby-throated Hummingbird ... 31
- [ ] Rufous Hummingbird ... 31
- [ ] Sandhill Crane ... 43
- [ ] Savannah Sparrow ... 19
- [ ] Scarlet Tanager ... 22
- [ ] Semipalmated Plover ... 36
- [ ] Short-eared Owl ... 35
- [ ] Snow Goose ... 38
- [ ] Snowy Egret ... 43
- [ ] Song Sparrow ... 19
- [ ] Spotted Sandpiper ... 37
- [ ] Steller's Jay ... 24
- [ ] Tree Swallow ... 28
- [ ] Tufted Titmouse ... 14
- [ ] Turkey Vulture ... 35
- [ ] Western Bluebird ... 13
- [ ] Western Tanager ... 22
- [ ] White-breasted Nuthatch ... 15
- [ ] White-throated Sparrow ... 19
- [ ] Wild Turkey ... 45
- [ ] Wilson's Warbler ... 17
- [ ] Wood Duck ... 38
- [ ] Yellow Warbler ... 16
- [ ] Yellow-headed Blackbird ... 27
- [ ] Yellow-rumped Warbler ... 18

How to Watch Birds

There are lots of ways to watch birds. You can move around or sit still. You can use only your eyes and ears, or you can see up close with binoculars. You can look out your window, visit a nature preserve, or notice birds as you roam your neighborhood. You can bird for five minutes or all day. The right way is whatever way makes you happy.

In this book are 100 North American birds to find, and 100 bird stickers. **When you see a bird, place its sticker next to its profile.** You'll spot some birds in your yard or local park. For others, you may need to visit a forest, beach, or other special habitat. Most of the birds (but not all) will spend time in your area, whether for a season or all year. Some birds, like the American Robin, you may find right away. And some, like the Belted Kingfisher, can take longer to locate. (But are totally worth the wait.)

As you **Seek-and-Sticker** the birds in this book, you'll get to know the secret world of nature, and the amazing animal lives happening all around you.

Using this Book

1. Begin by flipping through the book. Check out the bird pictures. Notice birds that seem familiar, and birds you really want to see.

2. Then, go out and look for birds. Try your local park or yard, to start. (Especially if there's a bird feeder.) Ask a family member or friend to join in—two people will see more than one. Only go where you know you're allowed, and if you're not sure, check with an adult.

When you see a bird, ask yourself three things:

- **What color is the bird?** If it's more than one color, where is each color on its body? (For example, a bird might have a gray back and head, and a white belly.)

- **What size and shape is it?** Does it look smaller than this book? Taller than your head? Bigger than other birds near it? Is its beak skinny, or chunky and triangular? Does it have a long or short tail?

- **What is it doing?** Is it pecking at the ground? Walking up a tree's trunk? Swimming in a lake? Stealing someone's french fries?

3. Flip through again and see if the bird you've spotted is in this book. If it is: sticker time! Find the bird's sticker at the back of the book, and stick it on the page next to the bird's profile. Not every bird you see will be in this book, but every bird is worth celebrating!

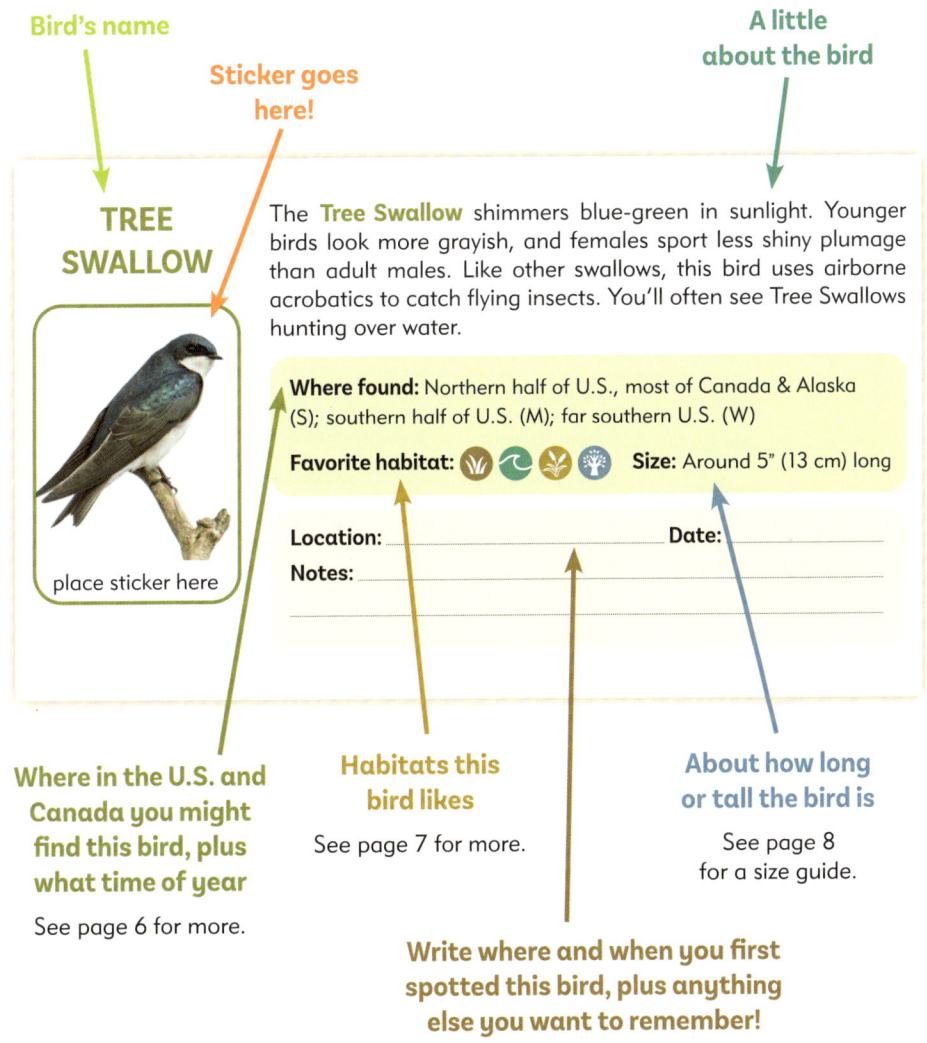

Bird's name

Sticker goes here!

A little about the bird

TREE SWALLOW

place sticker here

The **Tree Swallow** shimmers blue-green in sunlight. Younger birds look more grayish, and females sport less shiny plumage than adult males. Like other swallows, this bird uses airborne acrobatics to catch flying insects. You'll often see Tree Swallows hunting over water.

Where found: Northern half of U.S., most of Canada & Alaska (S); southern half of U.S. (M); far southern U.S. (W)

Favorite habitat: **Size:** Around 5" (13 cm) long

Location: _____ **Date:** _____
Notes: _____

Where in the U.S. and Canada you might find this bird, plus what time of year

See page 6 for more.

Habitats this bird likes

See page 7 for more.

About how long or tall the bird is

See page 8 for a size guide.

Write where and when you first spotted this bird, plus anything else you want to remember!

5

Where Birds Live

Not many birds live everywhere in North America. Famous birds like the Northern Cardinal and Steller's Jay are common in some places but absent from others. Most birds in this book will at least visit your area, but not all.

To see whether you might spot a bird near you, check its **where found** section. If you're still not sure, ask an adult. You can also search online for a detailed map of the bird's range.

Migration

Some birds live in the same place all year round. But many spend different seasons in different places. In winter lots of birds go farther south, where it's warm and food is plentiful. In spring they may head north, where they'll nest and stay all summer before heading south again in autumn. Migrating birds often stop along the way to rest and eat, so spring and autumn are exciting times. Unusual birds might visit your area while traveling to their summer or winter home!

In the **where found** section, you'll see letters next to different locations. The letters tell you **what time of year** to look for the bird in each region:

YR: Year-round

S: Summer season; usually the bird is there from spring to fall

M: Migration season(s); usually the bird will visit in spring and/or fall

W: Winter season; usually the bird is there from late fall to early spring

Habitats

A bird's habitat is the type of environment where it usually lives. The right habitat will offer the bird things like food, safety, and maybe a place to nest. Below each bird's description, these icons show its **favorite habitat:**

- **Shore and open water.** Try beaches, lakes, big rivers, and the ocean.

- **Wetlands.** Try freshwater and salt marshes, swamps, and bogs.

- **Forest.** Some birds prefer particular types or sizes of trees.

- **Grasslands, meadows, fields, sometimes farms.** Places with tall native grasses are often best.

- **Bushes and scrublands.** May be forest edges/clearings, berry bushes, and/or open areas with low brushy plants.

- **Backyards, parks, suburbs, and even some cities.** These birds often visit feeders.

- **Near people.** These birds often nest around buildings and/or eat things that humans leave out.

How Big Is that Bird?

Humans come in different sizes, and birds of the same species aren't all the same size either. But it helps to know a bird's average size, so below each bird's description you'll see roughly **how big** it is in inches and centimeters. Because it's hard to picture what 6 inches (15 cm) looks like, especially from far away, here's how birds of different sizes compare to the size of this book:

Birds of Many Feathers

Some birds look the same all year round. Males and females of many bird species appear similar or identical. But some birds look completely different depending on the season, their age, and whether they're female or male.

Male birds often (but not always!) look flashier. Their fancy feathers tell mates and rivals about their health, what they've been eating, and other things. Female birds often (but not always!) look more subtle, with colors that blend into the forest, marsh, or other habitat. Young birds may also have muted colors, and patterns that help them hide.

Some birds (male and female) grow brighter plumage for breeding season, then exchange it for more camouflage-friendly feathers as winter approaches. The American Goldfinch (page 20) is famous for this—some beginning birders are surprised to learn that the brown finches at their feeder in January are the same as the yellow birds that visited in June.

This book shows one easy-to-recognize picture of each bird, but that's often not the only way the bird can look. Check the descriptions for key facts about alternate appearances, and look online for more photos and ID tips.

Bird-Friendly Birding

It's tempting to get as close to birds as possible. But you'll see more interesting things if birds are relaxed and focused on bird stuff, instead of worried that you're about to pounce on them. **Give a bird space,** and you may see it sing, fight, eat, feed its babies, take a bath, scratch its head with its foot, and more.

Space is really important for nesting birds, and sensitive birds like owls. If you're watching a nest and a parent bird stares at you or seems stressed, back up. The same goes for owls. Most owls sleep on a hidden perch during the day. It's important not to scare them and make them leave their safe spot.

Binoculars or Not?

You don't need binoculars to enjoy birds. But you'll see more by using them, and spot things you might not otherwise. To find a bird with your binoculars, first stare at it with your eyes. Without moving your gaze, lift the binoculars up to your face. Slowly turn the focus knob until the bird is clear. This may take a little practice, but you'll get it!

Other Resources

Field Guides
These books are great references. They show different ways each bird can look, essential info, and range maps.

The Sibley Guide to Birds, by David Allen Sibley (app also available)
Kaufman Field Guide to Birds of North America, by Kenn Kaufman
Peterson Field Guide to Birds of North America, by Roger Tory Peterson (app also available)

Online Bird Guides
These websites offer details about the life of each bird, amazing images, and tips for beginning birders.

www.allaboutbirds.org
www.audubon.org

Apps for Birders
Merlin Bird ID helps you figure out what bird you saw. It can also identify birds from images and sounds, and keep a record of your sightings.
iNaturalist isn't just for birds—it helps you identify pretty much anything you see in nature.
The **eBird** app lets you log and share your bird sightings. It's also great for finding places to bird, taking part in bird events, and even looking up where a particular bird has appeared in your area. You can also use eBird via the web at **ebird.org**.

Other Tools
BirdCast is like a weather forecast for migrating birds. In spring and fall, it predicts when lots of cool birds may pass through your area. Check the **birdcast.info** website during the migration seasons, and if your part of the country "lights up" on the map, head out to see some birds!

AMERICAN ROBIN

American Robins can live nearly everywhere, from cities to forests. When the weather is warm, you'll probably see them hopping across the ground in search of bugs and worms. In winter, look for American Robins in trees and bushes that bear fruits or berries.

Where found: Most of U.S. (YR); Canada & Alaska (S)

Favorite habitat: **Size:** Around 9" (23 cm) long

Location: _____ Date: _____
Notes: _____

HERMIT THRUSH

You'll probably hear the **Hermit Thrush** before you see it. Its flute-like, haunting song is easy to recognize. (Try listening to a recording online.) This bird likes forests. Look for it in the low and middle branches of trees, and on the forest floor.

Where found: Northern & western U.S., southern Canada & Alaska (S); central U.S. (M); southern & West Coast U.S. (W)

Favorite habitat: **Size:** Around 6" (15 cm) long

Location: _____ Date: _____
Notes: _____

EASTERN BLUEBIRD

Humans help the **Eastern Bluebird** by putting up nest boxes. If you see a box on a post in a field, Eastern Bluebirds may be nearby. They like open areas full of bugs to eat, such as meadows and farms. When it gets cold, you can find them snacking on fruit trees and bushes, too.

Where found: Northeastern & north central U.S., southeastern & central Canada (S); southeastern & south central U.S. (YR)

Favorite habitat: **Size:** Around 7" (18 cm) long

Location: _____ Date: _____
Notes: _____

The **Mountain Bluebird** frequents open fields filled with tasty bugs, and often nests in boxes put up by humans (much like its relative, the Eastern Bluebird, on the previous page). Grassy or brush-filled places and farms are good spots to find this bird. It's at home in the mountains, but it likes lowland habitats, too.

Where found: Northwestern interior U.S. & Canada (S); southwestern interior U.S. (W & YR)

Favorite habitat: 🌿 🌐   **Size:** Around 7" (18 cm) long

Location: _____   Date: _____
Notes: _____

MOUNTAIN BLUEBIRD

The **Western Bluebird** has lots in common with the related Eastern Bluebird and Mountain Bluebird (above and previous page), including its favorite food types and nesting spots. You're more likely to find this bluebird near forests, though. It prefers spots with both trees and open areas, and places where a forest meets a field.

Where found: Northwestern interior U.S. (S & YR); southwestern U.S. (W & YR)

Favorite habitat: 🌳 🌿 🌐   **Size:** Around 7" (18 cm) long

Location: _____   Date: _____
Notes: _____

WESTERN BLUEBIRD

Tiny **Black-capped Chickadees** have big voices! They often move in groups, calling back and forth to one another. Look for their little round bodies, long tails, and black-and-white heads. Chickadees make lots of sounds but are famous for their alarm call: *chicka-dee-dee-dee*. They like habitats with trees, from forests to backyards.

Where found: Northern half of U.S., southern half of Canada & Alaska (YR)

Favorite habitat: 🌳 🌐 🏠   **Size:** Around 5" (13 cm) long

Location: _____   Date: _____
Notes: _____

BLACK-CAPPED CHICKADEE

CAROLINA CHICKADEE

The **Carolina Chickadee** looks a lot like the Black-capped Chickadee (previous page) but lives farther south. (Location is usually the best way to tell the two apart.) It often shows up at bird feeders, sometimes in flocks. Listen for its *chicka-dee-dee-dee* alarm call. In spring, this bird nests in a hole in a tree.

Where found: Southeastern & south central U.S. (YR)

Favorite habitat: 🌳 🌐 🏠   **Size:** Around 5" (13 cm) long

Location: _____   **Date:** _____
Notes: _____
_____

TUFTED TITMOUSE

The loudmouthed **Tufted Titmouse** is fun to watch. It can get feisty toward other birds, and sometimes harasses predators like hawks. It makes a variety of (usually noisy) calls and songs. The Tufted Titmouse likes to eat from bird feeders, especially if they're near a wooded area.

Where found: Eastern half of U.S. (YR)

Favorite habitat: 🌳 🏠   **Size:** Around 6" (15 cm) long

Location: _____   **Date:** _____
Notes: _____
_____

BUSHTIT

Bushtits move around in big groups, often of twenty or more. Look for tiny gray-brown birds with long tails, bouncing around like table tennis balls. Listen for high-pitched notes as they call to one another. Bushtits mostly eat bugs. They often visit yards and parks with trees.

Where found: West Coast & some southwestern U.S. (YR)

Favorite habitat: 🌳 🌐 🏠   **Size:** Around 4" (10 cm) long

Location: _____   **Date:** _____
Notes: _____
_____

White-breasted Nuthatches often walk down tree trunks head-first, searching the tree bark for tasty bugs. These birds also eat lots of seeds, and will snack from feeders. The White-breasted Nuthatch is larger than the Red-breasted Nuthatch (below), with a white face and chest.

Where found: Most of U.S. & some southern Canada (YR)

Favorite habitat: 🌳 🏠   **Size:** Around 6" (15 cm) long

Location: _____ Date: _____
Notes: _____

WHITE-BREASTED NUTHATCH

The **Red-breasted Nuthatch** is often seen moving back and forth around tree trunks, looking for food. Like the White-breasted Nuthatch (above), it eats bugs and seeds, and will wedge seeds into cracks in tree bark. It has a reddish-brown underside and a black stripe through its eye.

Where found: Northern & western U.S., southern half of Canada, southern Alaska (YR); southern & central U.S., some Canada (W)

Favorite habitat: 🌳 🏠   **Size:** Around 5" (13 cm) long

Location: _____ Date: _____
Notes: _____

RED-BREASTED NUTHATCH

The little **Brown Creeper** blends in so well, it looks like a moving piece of tree bark. It walks around tree trunks and branches, often in a spiral from bottom to top, seeking delicious bugs. Woods full of big, tall trees are your best bet for spotting this bird.

Where found: Northern & western U.S., southern & western Canada, southern Alaska (YR); southern & central U.S., Canada (W)

Favorite habitat: 🌳   **Size:** Around 5" (13 cm) long

Location: _____ Date: _____
Notes: _____

BROWN CREEPER

HOUSE WREN

Like most wrens, the **House Wren** often points its tail upward. (A wren's easiest "tell" is its jaunty tail.) This medium-brown little bird has subtle barred (striped) markings and a curved bill. It likes a bunch of habitats, including parks and yards—anywhere with bugs to eat and holes to nest in.

Where found: Far southern U.S. (W); mid-southern U.S. (M); northern ⅔ of U.S., southern Canada (S)

Favorite habitat: 　　　　　　　　　**Size:** Around 5" (13 cm) long

Location: _____ Date: _____

Notes: _____

MARSH WREN

The **Marsh Wren** flits and forages among marsh reeds and other plants near water. Listen for its complex song, full of buzzes and trills. Like other wrens, it has a curved bill and tends to point its tail upward.

Where found: East Coast & western U.S. (YR); southern U.S. (W); southeastern & western interior U.S. (M); northern U.S. & southern Canada (S)

Favorite habitat: 　　　　　　　　　**Size:** Around 5" (13 cm) long

Location: _____ Date: _____

Notes: _____

YELLOW WARBLER

The **Yellow Warbler** is one of the easiest warblers to find. Most of its body is yellow, with darker feathers on its wings and back, and reddish stripes on the male's chest. Like other warblers, it has a slim and straight beak, which it uses to eat bugs.

Where found: Most of U.S., Canada, and Alaska (S); southern U.S. (M)

Favorite habitat: 　　　　　　　　　**Size:** Around 5" (13 cm) long

Location: _____ Date: _____

Notes: _____

Black-and-white Warblers climb up, down, and around tree trunks and branches, seeking hidden bugs to munch. This pinstriped warbler can be easier to spot than other warblers because it forages closer to eye level. Search for it in woods, especially where there are large trees.

Where found: Northeastern & central U.S., southeastern & central Canada (S); southeastern & central U.S. (M & W)

Favorite habitat: 🌳   **Size:** Around 5" (13 cm) long

Location: _____ **Date:** _____
Notes: _____

BLACK-AND-WHITE WARBLER

place sticker here

A male **Wilson's Warbler** wears a fancy hat: a black spot right on top of its head! Female and young male Wilson's Warblers have more subtle feathers, and no black spot. The edges of woodlands are good places to seek out this always-moving bird.

Where found: Most of U.S., southern Canada (M); West Coast & northwestern U.S., most of Canada & Alaska (S)

Favorite habitat: 🌳 🌿   **Size:** Around 4" (10 cm) long

Location: _____ **Date:** _____
Notes: _____

WILSON'S WARBLER

place sticker here

The **American Redstart** is a bold little warbler, with bright colors to match its personality. Males are black with red markings around their wings and tail feathers, while females and young males are gray and yellow. If you're lucky, you may see this bird snatch a flying bug out of the air.

Where found: Eastern half of U.S., northwestern interior U.S, southern half of Canada (S); central & southern U.S. (M)

Favorite habitat: 🌳 🌿   **Size:** Around 5" (13 cm) long

Location: _____ **Date:** _____
Notes: _____

AMERICAN REDSTART

place sticker here

YELLOW-RUMPED WARBLER

The **Yellow-rumped Warbler** is nicknamed "butter-butt" for the yellow patch on its behind. Its markings can vary a lot, so look for that yellow butt patch. Warblers mostly eat bugs, and in summer, this bird is no exception. But in colder months, the Yellow-rumped Warbler can also eat fruit.

Where found: Far western U.S. (YR); southern & central U.S. (W); central U.S. & Canada (M); northern & western U.S., most of Canada, most of Alaska (S)

Favorite habitat: 🌳 🌐   **Size:** Around 5" (13 cm) long

Location: _____ Date: _____
Notes: _____

COMMON YELLOWTHROAT

The male **Common Yellowthroat** has a black mask over his face, like a raccoon's. Females lack the mask, and have less flashy colors overall. This warbler hunts for bugs in vegetation from trees to marsh grasses. Males sing a lot, so learning this bird's song can prove especially helpful.

Where found: Most of U.S. & southern half of Canada (S); southwestern U.S. (M); southeastern U.S. (YR)

Favorite habitat: 🌳 🌿 🌐 🌾   **Size:** Around 5" (13 cm) long

Location: _____ Date: _____
Notes: _____

GOLDEN-CROWNED KINGLET

The **Golden-crowned Kinglet** is a tiny bird with a big attitude! Its "crown" is a yellow stripe atop its head. During winter, you may spot flocks of kinglets foraging in trees, peeping to one another as they go. (In summer they're usually in pairs or alone.) They mostly eat bugs.

Where found: Southern & central U.S. (W); western northeastern U.S., coastal Canada, southern Alaska (YR); southern half of Canada (S)

Favorite habitat: 🌳 🌿 🌐 🏠   **Size:** Around 4" (10 cm) long

Location: _____ Date: _____
Notes: _____

The **Song Sparrow's** color can differ depending on your location. Look for thick streaky markings on its chest, often with a dark splotch in the middle. This common sparrow perches in plain sight to sing. It eats many things, and may visit your feeder.

Where found: Southern & central U.S. (W); central & northern U.S., western Canada, southern Alaska (YR); northern U.S., southern half of Canada (S)

Favorite habitat: 🌲 🌾 ⚪ 🏠 🌱   **Size:** Around 6" (15 cm) long

Location: _____ **Date:** _____
Notes: _____
_____

SONG SPARROW

Seek the **Savannah Sparrow** in grassy or brushy places, from meadows to farmland. Look for the yellow stripe over its eye, like an eyebrow. The streaks on its chest are thin, like they've been drawn on with a pencil. This sparrow eats bugs and seeds.

Where found: Southern U.S. (W); central U.S. (M); northern U.S., most of Canada, Alaska (S)

Favorite habitat: 🌾 ⚪   **Size:** Around 5" (13 cm) long

Location: _____ **Date:** _____
Notes: _____
_____

SAVANNAH SPARROW

The **White-throated Sparrow** has a little white chin, true to its name. White or tan stripes crown its head, and there's a yellow patch above its eye. In summer it's a forest bird, but in winter it frequents many habitats, and may stop at your backyard feeder.

Where found: Coastal, southern, & central U.S. (W); central & northwestern U.S., southwestern Canada (M); northern U.S, southern & central Canada (S)

Favorite habitat: 🌲 🌾 ⚪ 🏠   **Size:** Around 7" (18 cm) long

Location: _____ **Date:** _____
Notes: _____
_____

WHITE-THROATED SPARROW

DARK-EYED JUNCO

The **Dark-eyed Junco** is a sparrow in a tuxedo. Look for its dark head and back, white underside, and short pink bill. In the West, this bird typically has a brownish/tan back and sides. It likes various habitats, including yards, and will eat seeds from feeders.

Where found: Most of U.S. (W); western & northeastern U.S., coastal Canada (YR); most of Canada, most of Alaska (S)

Favorite habitat: 🌳 🌿 🌰 🏠   **Size:** Around 6" (15 cm) long

Location: _____   **Date:** _____
Notes: _____

HOUSE SPARROW

The **House Sparrow** is an introduced species. Imported from Europe in the 1800s, it has spread far and wide. It's not closely related to native North American sparrows. This bird lives where people live, can even thrive in cities, and enthusiastically eats from bird feeders.

Where found: Entire U.S., southern half of Canada (YR)

Favorite habitat: 🏠 🏙️   **Size:** Around 6" (15 cm) long

Location: _____   **Date:** _____
Notes: _____

AMERICAN GOLDFINCH

The **American Goldfinch** is famed for its sunny color. In warm months, males are bright yellow with black wings and caps, while females' colors are less intense. As summer ends, these birds swap their gold plumage for brownish winter feathers. They eat lots of seeds, and will snack from feeders.

Where found: Southern U.S. (W); central & northern U.S. (YR); northern U.S. & southern Canada (S)

Favorite habitat: 🌳 🌿 🌰 🏠   **Size:** Around 5" (13 cm) long

Location: _____   **Date:** _____
Notes: _____

The male **House Finch** looks like it was dipped headfirst in red paint, while the feathers of female and young birds are shades of brown. This common finch is native to the Southwest, was introduced in the East, and has spread across the U.S. House Finches frequently visit seed feeders.

Where found: Most of U.S., southern Canada (YR)

Favorite habitat: 🌳 🌾 🌐 🏠 👥   **Size:** Around 5" (13 cm) long

Location: _____ Date: _____
Notes: _____

HOUSE FINCH

place sticker here

The **Pine Siskin** is a brown-streaked bird with hints of flashy yellow. It's most often seen in flocks, searching the branches of conifer trees for tasty seeds. Look for Pine Siskins amid conifer forests, especially in winter. They may also stop by feeders stocked with small seeds.

Where found: Most of U.S. (W); western & northern U.S., southern & coastal Canada (YR); central Canada & Alaska (S)

Favorite habitat: 🌳 🌐 🏠   **Size:** Around 5" (13 cm) long

Location: _____ Date: _____
Notes: _____

PINE SISKIN

place sticker here

Male **Northern Cardinals** are bright red, and often seen sitting on branches, whistling their loud song. Female cardinals are warm brown, with a little red here and there. These birds eat lots of seeds and fruit. They frequently visit bird feeders!

Where found: Eastern, central, & southwestern U.S. (YR)

Favorite habitat: 🌳 🌐 🏠   **Size:** Around 9" (23 cm) long

Location: _____ Date: _____
Notes: _____

NORTHERN CARDINAL

place sticker here

SCARLET TANAGER

The male **Scarlet Tanager** is RED! In spring and summer he's a super-intense crimson, with black wings. Females and non-breeding males have yellow-green plumage, which offers great camouflage in the treetops. You may spot this bird hunting bugs among high branches.

Where found: Northeastern & central U.S. (S); southeastern & central U.S. (M)

Favorite habitat: 🌳   **Size:** Around 7" (18 cm) long

Location: _____ Date: _____
Notes: _____

WESTERN TANAGER

The adult male **Western Tanager** has an ombré look, with a yellow body shading to an orange head. Females are a leafy yellow-green, while young males are yellow and black. This bird eats a ton of insects. Look for it in forests, especially ones full of conifer trees.

Where found: Western U.S., western Canada (S); southwestern & central U.S. (M)

Favorite habitat: 🌳   **Size:** Around 7" (18 cm) long

Location: _____ Date: _____
Notes: _____

INDIGO BUNTING

The **Indigo Bunting** is named for the male's incredible blue color, which is easiest to see in bright light. He sings loudly and at length. Females and non-breeding males are a warm brown. Farmland is a good place to find this bird. Indigo Buntings may eat seed from feeders.

Where found: Eastern half of U.S., southwestern U.S., southeastern Canada (S)

Favorite habitat: 🌳 🌿 🌾   **Size:** Around 5" (13 cm) long

Location: _____ Date: _____
Notes: _____

"Grosbeak" means "big beak," and the **Rose-breasted Grosbeak** has a very chunky bill. This bigmouth sings a high, pretty song. The male is black on top and white below, with a hot pink chest. Females have a brown back, a yellowish underside, and a sharp white stripe above the eye.

ROSE-BREASTED GROSBEAK

place sticker here

Where found: Northeastern & central U.S., southern Canada (S); southeastern & central U.S. (M)

Favorite habitat: 🌳 🌐   **Size:** Around 8" (20 cm) long

Location: _____ **Date:** _____
Notes: _____

The **Black-headed Grosbeak** has much in common with the Rose-breasted Grosbeak (above), including a pretty voice. Females of the two species look similar. Breeding male Black-headed Grosbeaks have an orange chest, black and white wings and tail, and (of course) a black head.

BLACK-HEADED GROSBEAK

place sticker here

Where found: Western & central U.S., southwestern Canada (S); southwestern U.S. (M)

Favorite habitat: 🌳 🌿 🌐   **Size:** Around 7" (18 cm) long

Location: _____ **Date:** _____
Notes: _____

The **Blue Jay** is loud, flashy, and fun. Its bold personality and intelligence lead to many avian antics. Blue Jays make all kinds of sounds, and can mimic other birds' calls or even human noises. They eat many things, including seeds and suet from feeders, and they especially like acorns.

BLUE JAY

place sticker here

Where found: Eastern half of U.S., southern Canada (YR)

Favorite habitat: 🌳 🏠   **Size:** Around 11" (28 cm) long

Location: _____ **Date:** _____
Notes: _____

STELLER'S JAY

The clever **Steller's Jay** looks like it's been dip dyed, with feathers shading from black to brilliant blue. This bird's harsh call can be heard in habitats from city parks and backyards to deep forests. Like Blue Jays (previous page), they'll eat whatever they can get, and flock to seed or suet feeders.

Where found: Western U.S. & Canada (YR)

Favorite habitat: 🌳 🏠   **Size:** Around 12" (30 cm) long

Location: _____   **Date:** _____
Notes: _____

AMERICAN CROW

American Crows have serious smarts. They can thrive almost anywhere, from busy streets to wild woods to beaches. These sociable birds live in family groups and big flocks. They chat using a large vocabulary of calls, including the famous *caw!* Crows eat lots of stuff, and may snag nuts or suet from feeders.

Where found: Most of U.S., west coast of Canada (YR); southern half of Canada (S)

Favorite habitat: 🌳 🌾 🥜 🏠 👥 🌊 🌱   **Size:** Around 18" (46 cm) long

Location: _____   **Date:** _____
Notes: _____

COMMON RAVEN

The **Common Raven** is way bigger than a crow. Ravens also have a chunkier beak, and a diamond-shaped tail that can be seen in flight. While crows *caw*, ravens tend to *croak*. (And make plenty of other sounds, too!) Like their relatives, ravens are amazingly brainy, and their behavior can be fun to watch.

Where found: Western & northern U.S., most of Canada, Alaska (YR)

Favorite habitat: 🌳 🌾 🥜 🌊   **Size:** Around 25" (64 cm) long

Location: _____   **Date:** _____
Notes: _____

What does a **Northern Mockingbird** sound like? Almost anything! This talented mimic sings a series of ten or more mini-songs, often including imitations of other birds' songs, human sounds, and more. Each mockingbird's song medley is unique. They keep singing well past the dawn chorus, sometimes into evening.

Where found: Most of U.S., far southern Canada (YR)

Favorite habitat: **Size:** Around 9" (23 cm) long

Location: _____ Date: _____
Notes: _____

NORTHERN MOCKINGBIRD

place sticker here

The **Gray Catbird** really does *meow*. If you hear a catlike cry from the bushes, this bird may be near. It can also imitate other birds' songs and other sounds, like the related Northern Mockingbird (above). But the snippets it sings are shorter, and it doesn't repeat them.

Where found: Most of interior U.S., southern Canada (S); East Coast U.S. (YR); Gulf Coast U.S. (W)

Favorite habitat: **Size:** Around 9" (23 cm) long

Location: _____ Date: _____
Notes: _____

GRAY CATBIRD

place sticker here

The **Common Grackle's** voice sounds like a rusty metal hinge. These clever birds can thrive in many habitats, and often hang out in a flock. Their black feathers may appear iridescent, like an oil slick, in bright light. Look for their pale yellow eyes. Grackles often eat seed from feeders.

Where found: Most of eastern U.S. (YR); northeastern & central U.S., southern Canada (S)

Favorite habitat: **Size:** Around 12" (30 cm) long

Location: _____ Date: _____
Notes: _____

COMMON GRACKLE

place sticker here

RED-WINGED BLACKBIRD

When defending its territory, the **Red-winged Blackbird** may pick fights with much larger birds, or even swoop at humans! Males will perch up and scream their loud song, flashing their bright red shoulder patches. Females' plumage is patterned brown, with hints of orange. In spring and summer, many wetlands are full of these birds.

Where found: Most of U.S. (YR); northern U.S., southern half of Canada (S)

Favorite habitat: **Size:** Around 8" (20 cm) long

Location: _____ Date: _____
Notes: _____

BROWN-HEADED COWBIRD

Brown-headed Cowbirds once followed bison herds, laying their eggs in other birds' nests as they traveled. They've since spread across the continent, and still leave their young with other birds. (A large fledgling fed by a much smaller adult songbird is likely a baby cowbird.) Males are black with brown heads; females are brown all over.

Where found: Eastern, central, & West Coast U.S. (YR); northern U.S., interior western U.S., southern Canada (S)

Favorite habitat: **Size:** Around 7" (18 cm) long

Location: _____ Date: _____
Notes: _____

BREWER'S BLACKBIRD

In winter, **Brewer's Blackbirds** flock together. You may see big groups of iridescent black (male) and brown (female) birds searching the ground for seeds and other food, especially around farms. With its pale eyes, this bird may resemble the related Common Grackle (previous page). But it's differently shaped and much smaller.

Where found: Western U.S., British Columbia (YR); north central U.S., south central Canada (S); midwestern U.S. (M); southern U.S. (W)

Favorite habitat: **Size:** Around 9" (23 cm) long

Location: _____ Date: _____
Notes: _____

The **Baltimore Oriole** is all about orange. Adult males' plumage features ultra-bright orange; females and young males have subtler orange feathers; and when this bird is nearby, leaving out a sliced orange may attract it. Orioles love colorful ripe fruit. They also eat tons of bugs.

Where found: Northeastern & central U.S., southeastern & central Canada (S); southern & central U.S. (M); Florida (W)

Favorite habitat: 🌳   **Size:** Around 7" (18 cm) long

Location: _____ Date: _____
Notes: _____

BALTIMORE ORIOLE

place sticker here

The **Yellow-headed Blackbird** has a lot in common with the related Red-winged Blackbird (previous page). It also nests in wetlands, proclaims its territory with harsh singing, and fiercely fights off trespassers. Adult males have golden heads and chests. Females sport smaller yellow patches around the face and chest.

Where found: North central & western interior U.S., interior central & western Canada (S); central & southern U.S. (M & W)

Favorite habitat: 🌊 🌿   **Size:** Around 9" (23 cm) long

Location: _____ Date: _____
Notes: _____

YELLOW-HEADED BLACKBIRD

place sticker here

Cedar Waxwings have a berry good time together. Small flocks of these fruit-loving birds fly from tree to tree, plucking sweet treats. They call to each other with high-pitched whistles. They'll also catch insects in midair. If your yard or local park has fruit trees or berry bushes, waxwings may visit.

Where found: Northern half of U.S. (YR); southern half of U.S. (W); southern half of Canada (S)

Favorite habitat: 🌳 🌿   **Size:** Around 6" (15 cm) long

Location: _____ Date: _____
Notes: _____

CEDAR WAXWING

place sticker here

BARN SWALLOW

Look for **Barn Swallow** nests under the eaves of barns and houses, and in other sheltered spots on rural buildings. This agile bird hunts insects in fields and over water. It flies acrobatically, with quick swoops and turns. Its tail is much more deeply forked than other North American swallows' tails.

Where found: Most of U.S., southern half of Canada, southern Alaska (S)

Favorite habitat: **Size:** Around 7" (18 cm) long

Location: _____ Date: _____
Notes: _____

TREE SWALLOW

The **Tree Swallow** shimmers blue-green in sunlight. Younger birds look more grayish, and females sport less shiny plumage than adult males. Like other swallows, this bird uses airborne acrobatics to catch flying insects. You may see Tree Swallows hunting over water.

Where found: Northern U.S., most of Canada & Alaska (S); southern half of U.S. (M); far southern U.S. (W)

Favorite habitat: **Size:** Around 5" (13 cm) long

Location: _____ Date: _____
Notes: _____

EUROPEAN STARLING

The non-native **European Starling** was introduced to North America in the 1800s and spread across the continent. You may see huge starling flocks flying together in a "cloud" of birds. This bird will eat most things, including seeds or suet from feeders. It makes many sounds in its metallic voice, and can mimic.

Where found: Most of U.S., southern ¾ of Canada (YR)

Favorite habitat: **Size:** Around 8" (20 cm) long

Location: _____ Date: _____
Notes: _____

The plump **Mourning Dove** coos hauntingly from its perch: cooOOO, coo, coo, coo. (Some mistake its voice for an owl's.) When taking flight or landing, it may announce itself with a trill. This bird mostly forages for food on the ground. It will visit feeders, but prefers seed at ground level.

Where found: Most of U.S. (YR); northern U.S., southern Canada (S)

Favorite habitat: 🌳 🌾 🌿 🏠   **Size:** Around 11" (28 cm) long

Location: _____ **Date:** _____
Notes: _____

MOURNING DOVE

Rock Pigeons were once our pets. They've carried messages, competed in races, and more. Introduced to North America hundreds of years ago, they now live where people do. These doves are superstars at thriving alongside us, nesting on buildings and often eating our leftovers. Some people still keep pet pigeons today.

Where found: Entire U.S., southern Canada (YR)

Favorite habitat: 🏠 🏙️   **Size:** Around 13" (33 cm) long

Location: _____ **Date:** _____
Notes: _____

ROCK PIGEON

The black-and-white **Downy Woodpecker** is North America's littlest woodpecker, smaller and with a shorter bill than the very similar Hairy Woodpecker (next page). This bird spends much of its time hammering on tree trunks and branches to get at tasty bugs. It will eat other things as well, including suet.

Where found: Most of U.S., southern half of Canada, southern Alaska (YR)

Favorite habitat: 🌳 🌿 🏠   **Size:** Around 6" (15 cm) long

Location: _____ **Date:** _____
Notes: _____

DOWNY WOODPECKER

HAIRY WOODPECKER

The **Hairy Woodpecker** looks like a larger version of the Downy Woodpecker (previous page). Keep an eye out for the Hairy Woodpecker's longer bill. Like other woodpeckers, this bird wanders along tree trunks and branches, tap-tap-tapping to find bugs in and beneath the bark. Suet feeders may attract it.

Where found: Most of U.S., southern ¾ of Canada, southern & interior Alaska (YR)

Favorite habitat: 🌳 🏠   **Size:** Around 9" (23 cm) long

Location: _____ Date: _____
Notes: _____
_____

PILEATED WOODPECKER

The enormous **Pileated Woodpecker** is about the size of a crow. Listen for a deep *TOK, TOK, TOK* sound as it taps on wood. This bird prefers forests full of big trees. Like other woodpeckers, it often visits dead trees and large logs, attracted by the many delicious bugs that live in rotting wood.

Where found: Eastern half of U.S., northwestern U.S., some southern Canada (YR)

Favorite habitat: 🌳   **Size:** Around 18" (46 cm) long

Location: _____ Date: _____
Notes: _____
_____

NORTHERN FLICKER

The **Northern Flicker** boasts spots, stripes, and surprises. In eastern North America, flying Northern Flickers display brilliant yellow beneath their wings and tail; farther west, they flash vivid red instead. This woodpecker spends more time foraging on the ground than its relatives do.

Where found: Most of U.S., southern Canada (YR); most of Canada, interior Alaska (S)

Favorite habitat: 🌳 🌾 🌰 🏠   **Size:** Around 12" (30 cm) long

Location: _____ Date: _____
Notes: _____
_____

The **Red-bellied Woodpecker's** reddest feature is the scarlet cap atop its head. Like other woodpeckers, this bird is drawn to dead trees, which offer both bugs to eat and nesting space. When it's time to nest, woodpeckers usually carve out a cozy hollow in dead wood, and raise their babies inside.

Where found: Most of eastern half of U.S. (YR)

Favorite habitat: 🌳 🏠   **Size:** Around 9" (23 cm) long

Location: _____ **Date:** _____
Notes: _____

RED-BELLIED WOODPECKER

The tiny, feisty **Ruby-throated Hummingbird** is eastern North America's only hummingbird. Its back shines green, and the male has an iridescent red throat. Like other hummingbirds, it hovers in midair to sip sweet nectar from trumpet-shaped flowers. If you plant its favorite flowers or provide a sugar water feeder, it may visit!

Where found: Eastern half of U.S., southeastern Canada (S)

Favorite habitat: 🌳 🌿 🌸 🏠   **Size:** Around 3" (8 cm) long

Location: _____ **Date:** _____
Notes: _____

RUBY-THROATED HUMMINGBIRD

Rufous Hummingbirds are small even for hummingbirds, but super fierce. Females have green backs and pale undersides, while adult males have lots of coppery plumage and metallic red throats. In standard hummingbird fashion, they hover like helicopters to drink flowers' nectar (and sugar water from feeders).

Where found: Northwestern U.S., western Canada, far southern Alaska (S); western U.S. (M)

Favorite habitat: 🌳 🌿 🌸 🏠   **Size:** Around 3" (8 cm) long

Location: _____ **Date:** _____
Notes: _____

RUFOUS HUMMINGBIRD

RED-TAILED HAWK

If you see a big hawk in a tree or soaring, chances are it's a **Red-tailed Hawk**. Its namesake russet tail is easiest to see from behind/above. Red-tailed Hawks often have a pale underside with a "belt" of dark streaks. You may spot this bird hunting small animals, from mice and squirrels to snakes, often in open areas.

Where found: Most of U.S. (YR); northern U.S., most of Canada, southern & interior Alaska (S)

Favorite habitat: 🌳 🌾 ⚪ **Size:** Around 20" (51 cm) long

Location: _____ **Date:** _____
Notes: _____

COOPER'S HAWK

The **Cooper's Hawk** is crow-sized, with a dark back, flat-topped head, gray behind its neck, and reddish markings on its chest. (It looks similar to the smaller Sharp-shinned Hawk; experienced birders can help you tell the difference.) This raptor flies nimbly through the forest, hunting other birds.

Where found: Most of U.S. (YR); northern U.S. & some southern Canada (S); far southern U.S. (W)

Favorite habitat: 🌳 **Size:** Around 15" (38 cm) long

Location: _____ **Date:** _____
Notes: _____

NORTHERN HARRIER

The **Northern Harrier** flies low across fields and wetlands, hunting small animals. Look for this bird's slightly flat face, and the white patch at the base of its long tail. Full-grown males tend to have pale chests and gray backs, while females and young harriers are more brown.

Where found: Central & western U.S., west coast of Canada (YR); northern U.S., most of Canada & Alaska (S); southern & western U.S. (W)

Favorite habitat: 🌾 🌿 **Size:** Around 19" (48 cm) long

Location: _____ **Date:** _____
Notes: _____

The **Bald Eagle** was endangered, but recovered when humans took steps to protect our environment. Bald Eagles are some of the biggest birds around. They mostly eat fish, and like places with both tall perches and water for fishing. Try lakes, rivers, and beaches near woods.

Where found: Most of U.S. & southern Canada (W); coastal & some interior U.S., coastal Canada, southern coastal Alaska (YR); north midwestern U.S., most of Canada, interior Alaska (S)

Favorite habitat: **Size:** Around 3' (1 m) long

Location: _____ **Date:** _____
Notes: _____

BALD EAGLE

place sticker here

The teeny **American Kestrel** is our continent's smallest bird of prey. This mini-falcon mostly hunts bugs, and snatches flying insects out of the air. It likes open spaces with low plants, like fields and brush, plus a few taller perches. You may spot it sitting on a sign or fencepost.

Where found: Most of U.S. (YR); northern U.S., most of Canada, some Alaska (S); far southern U.S. (W)

Favorite habitat: **Size:** Around 10" (25 cm) long

Location: _____ **Date:** _____
Notes: _____

AMERICAN KESTREL

place sticker here

The **Peregrine Falcon** is the world's fastest animal. It hunts other birds by soaring above them, then diving down at incredible speed to snatch them out of the sky. This bird can thrive in cities, since tall buildings resemble the cliffs it likes to nest on, and pigeons are perfect prey.

Where found: Most of U.S. & Canada, southern Alaska (M); some coastal & interior U.S. (YR); some western U.S., northern Canada & Alaska (S); southern U.S. (W)

Favorite habitat: **Size:** Around 17" (43 cm) long

Location: _____ **Date:** _____
Notes: _____

PEREGRINE FALCON

place sticker here

MERLIN

The **Merlin** isn't a wizard. This falcon is about as big as a Mourning Dove (see p. 29), with plumage patterned densely in dark browns and/or grays. It hunts in open spaces, often catching other birds, and especially likes habitats near water.

Where found: Eastern & central U.S. (M); southern & western U.S. (W); northwestern U.S., far western Canada, southern Alaska (YR); northern U.S., most of Canada & Alaska (S)

Favorite habitat: 🌳 🌾 🌊 🍃 🌱   **Size:** Around 11" (28 cm) long

Location: _____ Date: _____

Notes: _____

OSPREY

The **Osprey** is sometimes called the "fish hawk." (Guess why.) Seek this bird pretty much anywhere with water full of fish. Many places have built special Osprey nest platforms; look for a pole with a huge pile of sticks atop it. Ospreys are large raptors with unusually long wings.

Where found: Eastern & northwestern U.S., most of Canada & Alaska (S); most interior U.S., some southern Canada (M); some coastal U.S. (YR & W)

Favorite habitat: 🌳 🌊 🌱   **Size:** Around 22" (56 cm) long

Location: _____ Date: _____

Notes: _____

GREAT HORNED OWL

Listen for the **Great Horned Owl's** deep-voiced hooting at dusk, nighttime, and dawn. This huge owl is a camouflage master. Look for its yellow eyes and the pair of tufts on its head. It perches high in trees and sleeps up there all day. Take care not to scare owls or get too close; see p. 10 for owl tips.

Where found: Most of U.S., Canada, and Alaska (YR)

Favorite habitat: 🌳   **Size:** Around 21" (53 cm) long

Location: _____ Date: _____

Notes: _____

The **Barred Owl's** hooting is higher than the Great Horned Owl's (previous page), and sounds a bit like *who-cooks-for-you?* This fluffy owl has huge black eyes, brown-striped plumage, and no head tufts. It hunts in the dark and sleeps in trees all day. Take care not to disturb owls; see p. 10 for owl tips.

Where found: Eastern half of U.S., northwestern U.S., southern & western Canada (YR)

Favorite habitat: 🌳 **Size:** Around 18" (46 cm) long

Location: _____ **Date:** _____
Notes: _____

BARRED OWL

place sticker here

The **Short-eared Owl** flies low over open spaces, hunting small animals. It's more active in daylight than most owls, especially near dawn and dusk. This brown-mottled bird is about as big as a Cooper's Hawk (see p. 32). Its yellow eyes are ringed with black, as though it's wearing eyeliner.

Where found: Southern ¾ of U.S. (W); Northern U.S. (YR); most of Canada & Alaska (S)

Favorite habitat: 🌿🌾🌱 **Size:** Around 15" (38 cm) long

Location: _____ **Date:** _____
Notes: _____

SHORT-EARED OWL

place sticker here

Turkey Vultures are nature's cleanup crew. When an animal dies, these huge scavengers take care of the mess by eating it. To avoid dirty feathers, their red heads are bald. You'll often see them near roads and open fields. They soar with their long black-and-gray wings in a V shape, rocking gently.

Where found: Most of U.S., southern Canada (S); southern U.S. (YR)

Favorite habitat: 🌳🌿🌾 **Size:** Around 29" (74 cm) long

Location: _____ **Date:** _____
Notes: _____

TURKEY VULTURE

place sticker here

BELTED KINGFISHER

The **Belted Kingfisher** perches over water and watches for fish. When it sees prey, it dives in beak-first and snags its meal. This bird has a large head, a long straight beak, and a spiky "hairdo" (a.k.a. crest). Listen for its loud rattling call.

Where found: Most of U.S., coastal Canada, southern Alaska (YR); northern U.S., most of Canada & Alaska (S); southern U.S. (W)

Favorite habitat: 🌊 🌾   **Size:** Around 12" (30 cm) long

Location: _____ Date: _____

Notes: _____

KILLDEER

Unlike many plovers, the **Killdeer** doesn't just live near water. This long-legged bird is at home in open fields as well as wetlands. It has a solid brown back, a white underside, black markings, and a red ring around its black eye. If you approach its nest, it may fake an injury to distract you from its babies.

Where found: Southern ⅔ of U.S., northwestern U.S. (YR); northern U.S., southern half of Canada (S)

Favorite habitat: 🌱 🌾 🌊   **Size:** Around 10" (25 cm) long

Location: _____ Date: _____

Notes: _____

SEMIPALMATED PLOVER

The **Semipalmated Plover** is littler and rounder than the Killdeer (above). It has a dark "mask" across its eye, and orange on its bill and legs. These shorebirds run around snagging small prey out of sand and mud. They like wetlands and beaches, but may also visit fields.

Where found: Most of U.S., southern half of Canada (M); coastal U.S. (W); northern & Maritime Canada, Alaska (S)

Favorite habitat: 🌱 🌊 🌾   **Size:** Around 7" (18 cm) long

Location: _____ Date: _____

Notes: _____

Look sharp for the **Spotted Sandpiper's** butt wiggle. It bobs its tail as it seeks small prey like bugs and snails. This sandpiper is spotted only in summer; in winter, it has a plain white underside and light brown back. Spotted Sandpipers prefer any habitat near water, from ponds to beaches.

> **Where found:** Northern ¾ of U.S., most of Canada & Alaska (S); southern U.S. (M & W)
>
> **Favorite habitat:** 🌊🌱   **Size:** Around 7" (18 cm) long

Location: _____ **Date:** _____

Notes: _____

SPOTTED SANDPIPER

The **Least Sandpiper** is the world's smallest shorebird. No bigger than a finch, this wader runs across wetlands and beaches on speedy little legs. It's often seen in flocks, picking through seaweed or perusing mud flats. Least Sandpipers have skinny black beaks, mottled brown backs, and white undersides.

> **Where found:** Northern ¾ of U.S., southern half of Canada (M); southern U.S. (W); northern & Maritime Canada, Alaska (S)
>
> **Favorite habitat:** 🌊🌱   **Size:** Around 5" (13 cm) long

Location: _____ **Date:** _____

Notes: _____

LEAST SANDPIPER

You may find the bold **Canada Goose** in almost any body of water, park, or field. These large geese eat mainly plants and seeds, including grass, and often graze on lawns and athletic fields. Don't feed them, as they can get aggressive. When raising babies, they'll hiss or even charge at people if approached.

> **Where found:** Most of northern U.S. (YR); southern U.S. (W); far northern U.S., most of Canada & Alaska (S)
>
> **Favorite habitat:** 🏞️🌊🌱🏙️   **Size:** Around 3' (1 m) long

Location: _____ **Date:** _____

Notes: _____

CANADA GOOSE

SNOW GOOSE

You may see huge flocks of **Snow Geese** during winter and migration. These stocky, mostly white geese breed in the Arctic, but fly south for the coldest months. They forage in wetlands, farm fields, and other open areas, usually near calm water. Look for them flying to their night roost around dusk.

Where found: Most of U.S., Canada, and Alaska (M); south central, East Coast, and some western U.S. (W); Arctic (S)

Favorite habitat: 　　　　　　　　**Size:** Around 30" (76 cm) long

Location: _____ Date: _____
Notes: _____

MALLARD

The **Mallard** is our most common duck, and can be seen almost anywhere there's water. Look for the male's shiny green head, the female's mottled brown feathers and orangish bill, and the blue patch on this large duck's wing. If you feed ducks, don't give them bread. Try oats, seeds, or vegetables instead.

Where found: Northern ⅔ of U.S., coastal Canada, southern Alaska (YR); southern U.S. (W); most of Canada & Alaska (S)

Favorite habitat: 　　　　　　　　**Size:** Around 22" (56 cm) long

Location: _____ Date: _____
Notes: _____

WOOD DUCK

The handsome **Wood Duck** loves freshwater wetlands. Adult male Wood Ducks have an iridescent green head with white markings, a reddish bill, and scarlet eyes. Females have soft brown plumage, with a white stripe and yellow ring around each dark eye. This duck forages both in and out of water.

Where found: Eastern half of U.S., northwestern & West Coast U.S. (YR); northern U.S. & southern Canada (S); south central & western U.S. (W)

Favorite habitat: 　　　　　　　　**Size:** Around 20" (51 cm) long

Location: _____ Date: _____
Notes: _____

Listen for the whistling chatter of **American Wigeons**. Breeding males have a shiny green "racing stripe" on their heads; females are patterned in grayish brown. These ducks often gather in big groups on the water, calling back and forth as they browse for food.

Where found: Coastal & south central U.S. (W); northwestern interior U.S., central & western Canada, most of Alaska (S); rest of U.S. (M)

Favorite habitat: 　　　　**Size:** Around 20" (51 cm) long

Location: _____ Date: _____
Notes: _____

AMERICAN WIGEON

place sticker here

The **Northern Shoveler** is literally a bigmouth. It uses its extra-large bill to sieve food out of the water. Adult males have a green head on a brown, white, and black body; females' plumage is patterned brown. Seek this duck in calm, often shallow waters.

Where found: Coastal, southern, & northwestern U.S. (W & YR); central U.S. & Canada, most of Alaska (S); rest of U.S. & southern Canada (M)

Favorite habitat: 　　　　**Size:** Around 19" (48 cm) long

Location: _____ Date: _____
Notes: _____

NORTHERN SHOVELER

place sticker here

The **Northern Pintail** is named for the male's long, gracefully pointed black tail. Males have a chocolate brown head, white neck, and gray body; females' feathers are prettily patterned in brown. This duck forages in fresh and salt water, as well as fields.

Where found: Coastal & southern U.S., west coast of Canada (W & YR); northern interior U.S., most of Canada & Alaska (S); rest of U.S. (M)

Favorite habitat: 　　**Size:** Around 21" (53 cm) long

Location: _____ Date: _____
Notes: _____

NORTHERN PINTAIL

place sticker here

RED-BREASTED MERGANSER

The **Red-breasted Merganser** dives for its dinner. Watch this duck plunge underwater, then reappear holding a fish or crab. Its bill is serrated like a bread knife, helping it grip its prey. Both males and females have feathery crests. The male's head is dark green, while the female's is reddish brown.

Where found: Coastal U.S. & Canada (W); interior U.S., southern & western Canada (M); rest of Canada & Alaska (S)

Favorite habitat: 🌊🌱   **Size:** Around 22" (56 cm) long

Location: _____ **Date:** _____
Notes: _____
_____

BUFFLEHEAD

The **Bufflehead** is North America's smallest duck, named for its (relatively) huge head. This bird dives underwater for shellfish and other small prey. The adult male's black and white head shines with rainbow iridescence in the sun. The female is mostly dark brown, with a white spot on her face.

Where found: Most of U.S., coastal Canada, south coast of Alaska (W); northern U.S., southern Alaska (M); interior Canada & Alaska (S)

Favorite habitat: 🌊🌱   **Size:** Around 14" (36 cm) long

Location: _____ **Date:** _____
Notes: _____
_____

AMERICAN COOT

The **American Coot** is a plump black bird with a tiny head, and maybe the weirdest feet you've ever seen. (Its extra-long "lobed" toes help it swim.) Look for this bird bobbing along and foraging for plants in wetlands, lakes, bays, and other calm water.

Where found: Western & south central U.S. (YR); southeastern U.S. & west coast of Canada (W); interior U.S. & southern half of Canada (S)

Favorite habitat: 🌊🌱   **Size:** Around 16" (41 cm) long

Location: _____ **Date:** _____
Notes: _____
_____

The petite **Pied-billed Grebe** dives underwater for any prey it can catch. This cute aquatic hunter has brown plumage, big dark eyes, and a super-short bill with a black stripe. (And weird feet, though you may not see them.) It prefers to fish in calm waters; fresh or salt will do.

Where found: Southern & western U.S. (YR); rest of U.S., southern & central Canada (S)

Favorite habitat: 🌊🌱 **Size:** Around 13" (33 cm) long

Location: _____ Date: _____
Notes: _____

PIED-BILLED GREBE

place sticker here

Look for **Double-crested Cormorants** sitting by the water with their wings open, drying in the sun. They're a bit clumsy on land but expert swimmers. This dark brown bird has orange on its face, and pretty green eyes. It likes waters deep enough to dive for fish, near rocks or trees to perch on.

Where found: Coastal & southern U.S., far western Canada, south coast of Alaska (W & YR); East Coast & interior U.S. & Canada (S); rest of U.S. (M)

Favorite habitat: 🌊🌱 **Size:** Around 30" (76 cm) long

Location: _____ Date: _____
Notes: _____

DOUBLE-CRESTED CORMORANT

place sticker here

The gangly **Great Blue Heron** stands taller than many kids. It wades through water, searching for fish to snap up with its long sharp beak. (It also hunts amphibians, mammals, and any other prey it can swallow. Plus some prey it can't swallow, but will try to gulp down anyway.)

Where found: Most of U.S., west coast of Canada, south coast of Alaska (YR); interior U.S. & southern Canada (M & S)

Favorite habitat: 🌾🌊🌱 **Size:** Around 4' (1.2 m) tall

Location: _____ Date: _____
Notes: _____

GREAT BLUE HERON

place sticker here

GREEN HERON

The little **Green Heron** has a grumpy expression. It tends to wade, or cling to a branch above the water, hunched over and watching for fish. Then it strikes, extending its surprisingly long neck. Green Herons like wetlands with trees and other plants to perch and hide in.

Where found: Eastern half of U.S., West Coast U.S. (S); southern U.S. (YR); southwestern U.S. (W & M)

Favorite habitat: **Size:** Around 17" (43 cm) long

Location: _____ Date: _____
Notes: _____

BLACK-CROWNED NIGHT HERON

When darkness falls, the **Black-crowned Night Heron** emerges to hunt. This black and white wading bird stalks small wetland creatures by night, then spends the day resting. In daylight, look for it perched quietly near water, perhaps on a branch. Dusk is a good time to spot it in action.

Where found: Most of U.S., south central Canada (S & YR); southwestern U.S. (W)

Favorite habitat: **Size:** Around 24" (61 cm) long

Location: _____ Date: _____
Notes: _____

GREAT EGRET

The all-white **Great Egret** strides through wetlands on skinny black legs, seeking prey with its sharp eyes and sharper beak. Like many of its heron relatives, it mostly hunts fish but isn't picky. In breeding season this bird shows off with fabulous fringed plumes.

Where found: Southern & coastal U.S. (YR & W); eastern half of U.S., some interior U.S., southeastern Canada (M & S)

Favorite habitat: **Size:** Around 3' (1 m) long

Location: _____ Date: _____
Notes: _____

To identify an adult **Snowy Egret**, check its feet. This wader's black legs end in bright yellow toes, as though it's wearing gold gloves. When breeding, the Snowy Egret grows luxurious fluffy plumage behind its head and on its back. It hunts small creatures in many wetland and shore habitats.

Where found: Northeast coastal & southern interior U.S. (M & S); southern coastal U.S. (YR)

Favorite habitat: 🌳 🌊 🌾   **Size:** Around 24" (61 cm) long

Location: _____ **Date:** _____
Notes: _____
_____

SNOWY EGRET

place sticker here

Migrating **Sandhill Cranes** are a majestic sight. They journey to and from their wintering grounds in flocks that can number thousands of birds. These tall, red-capped cranes frequent wetlands and open spaces near water. During winter you may spot them foraging in farm fields.

Where found: Northern U.S., most of Canada & Alaska (S); central U.S. (M); southern U.S. (W & YR)

Favorite habitat: 🌊 🌾   **Size:** Around 4' (1.2 m) tall

Location: _____ **Date:** _____
Notes: _____
_____

SANDHILL CRANE

place sticker here

The scrappy **Ring-billed Gull** can make it anywhere. It will gladly eat fish from the sea, bugs from the dirt, and even garbage from a dumpster. This mid-sized bird has yellow legs, yellow eyes, and a yellow beak with a black band. It's been voted "gull most likely to loiter outside a fast food restaurant."

Where found: Coastal & southern U.S. (W); northeastern & interior U.S. (M); northern U.S. & southern half of Canada (S & YR)

Favorite habitat: 🌊 🌾 🏙️ 🌾   **Size:** Around 18" (46 cm) long

Location: _____ **Date:** _____
Notes: _____
_____

RING-BILLED GULL

place sticker here

HERRING GULL

The hefty **Herring Gull** is bigger and stockier than the Ring-billed Gull (previous page). It has pale gray wings, yellow eyes, pink legs, and a yellow bill marked with a red dot. This gull eats aquatic animals, land bugs, and whatever else it can get (including your precious ice cream cone).

Where found: Northeast coastal U.S., most of Canada, southern Alaska (S & YR); coastal & eastern U.S. (W); rest of U.S. & Canada (M)

Favorite habitat: **Size:** Around 24" (61 cm) long

Location: _____ Date: _____
Notes: _____

BONAPARTE'S GULL

The trim **Bonaparte's Gull** hasn't embraced dumpster diving. It prefers to dive for fish, or catch other small prey. When breeding, this compact bird has a thin black bill, pinkish-red legs, and a black-capped head. (Outside of breeding season its head is white with a gray dot.)

Where found: Coastal & southeastern U.S. (W); rest of U.S., far western & southern Canada (M); interior Canada, southern Alaska (S)

Favorite habitat: **Size:** Around 11" (28 cm) long

Location: _____ Date: _____
Notes: _____

COMMON TERN

Common Terns are pointy all over. Pointy forked tail, long pointy wings, pointy black-tipped red beak. Telling them apart from other terns can be tricky, but gets easier with practice. Watch them swoop at the water, elegantly snagging fish and other aquatic prey.

Where found: Northern & East Coast U.S., southern & central Canada (S); most of U.S., southern Canada (M)

Favorite habitat: **Size:** Around 13" (33 cm) long

Location: _____ Date: _____
Notes: _____

The rotund **Wild Turkey** has long ruled the forest floor, and now roams some city streets too. From its insistent gobbling to its bulk, you can't miss this bird. Breeding males fan their tails and stick out their colorful bald heads to impress mates. In spring and summer, fluffy chicks trot behind their mothers.

Where found: Most of U.S. (YR)

Favorite habitat: 🌳

Size: Around 3' (1 m) long

Location: _____ **Date:** _____
Notes: _____

WILD TURKEY

place sticker here

LET'S GO FIND SOME AMAZING BIRDS!

PETER PAUPER PRESS

In 1928, at the age of twenty-two, Peter Beilenson began printing books on a small press in the basement of his parents' home in Larchmont, New York. Peter—and later, his wife, Edna—sought to create fine books that sold at "prices even a pauper could afford."

Today, still family owned and operated, Peter Pauper Press continues to honor our founders' legacy of quality, value, and fun for big kids and small kids alike.

This book was written on the land of the Coast Salish peoples.

Written by T. Levy

Designed by Keri Steckler

Artwork and photography used under license from Shutterstock.com

Copyright © 2023
Peter Pauper Press, Inc.
3 International Drive
Rye Brook, NY 10573 USA

Published in the United Kingdom and Europe by
Peter Pauper Press, Inc. c/o White Pebble International
Units 2-3, Spring Business Park
Stanbridge Road
Havant, Hampshire PO9 2GJ, UK

All rights reserved
ISBN 978-1-4413-4135-8
Printed in China

7 6 5 4 3 2 1

Visit us at www.peterpauper.com

Dark-eyed Junco (p. 20)

House Sparrow (p. 20)

American Goldfinch (p. 20)

House Finch (p. 21)

Pine Siskin (p. 21)

Northern Cardinal (p. 21)

Scarlet Tanager (p. 22)

Western Tanager (p. 22)

Indigo Bunting (p. 22)

Rose-breasted Grosbeak (p. 23)

Black-headed Grosbeak (p. 23)

Blue Jay (p. 23)

Steller's Jay (p. 24)

American Crow (p. 24)

Common Raven (p. 24)

Northern Mockingbird (p. 25)

Gray Catbird (p. 25)

Common Grackle (p. 25)

Red-winged Blackbird (p. 26)

Brown-headed Cowbird (p. 26)

Brewer's Blackbird (p. 26)

Baltimore Oriole (p. 27)

Yellow-headed Blackbird (p. 27)

Cedar Waxwing (p. 27)

Barn Swallow (p. 28)

Tree Swallow (p. 28)

European Starling (p. 28)

Mourning Dove (p. 29)

Rock Pigeon (p. 29)

Downy Woodpecker (p. 29)

Hairy Woodpecker (p. 30)

Pileated Woodpecker (p. 30)

Northern Flicker (p. 30)

Red-bellied Woodpecker (p. 31)

Ruby-throated Hummingbird (p. 31)

Rufous Hummingbird (p. 31)

Belted Kingfisher (p. 36)

Killdeer (p. 36)

Semipalmated Plover (p. 36)

Spotted Sandpiper (p. 37)

Least Sandpiper (p. 37)

Canada Goose (p. 37)

Snow Goose (p. 38)

Mallard (p. 38)

Wood Duck (p. 38)

American Wigeon (p. 39)

Northern Shoveler (p. 39)

Northern Pintail (p. 39)

Herring Gull (p. 44)

Bonaparte's Gull (p. 44)

Common Tern (p. 44)

Wild Turkey (p. 45)

I Spotted **25** Birds!

I Spotted **50** Birds!

I'm with the birds

follow that bird

Gone birding